NIGHTMARES #1

# DEATH SKETCH

**TOBIAS YOUNGBLOOD
& OLIVER SHADE**

# DEATH SKETCH

NIGHTMARES #1

**TOBIAS YOUNGBLOOD**

**OLIVER SHADE**

RIPOSTE

# JOIN THE YOUNGBLOOD NEWSLETTER

Members get free books, exclusive content, and first look at upcoming releases.

See the back of the book for details on how to join.

Copyright © 2023 by Tobias Youngblood & Oliver Shade

The moral right of Tobias Youngblood & Oliver Shade to be identified as the authors of this work has been asserted by them in accordance with the Copyright, Design and Patent Act 1988.

All events and characters in this book are fictitious, and any resemblance to actual persons or events is purely coincidental.

This novel was created by genuine humans. No A.I. was used in the drafting of this work.

All rights reserved.

No part of this publication may be reproduced, stored in a retrieval system or transmitted in any form or by any means, without the prior permission in writing of the publisher, except for the use of brief quotations in a book review.

Cover designed by Miblart.

Riposte Press

ISBN: 978-1-959649-04-5 (e-book)

ISBN: 978-1-959649-05-2 (Print)

# CHAPTER
# ONE

PAUL CRINGED when former colleague Johnny Briggs took the stage at the 78th annual Writers and Illustrators Conference. Briggs waved one hand at a large projector and a series of vivid, full-color illustrations appeared under the session title "Visuals Matter". Paul recognized the works on display—charcoal illustrations that had been scanned for digital manipulation. They were all pieces from Johnny's website.

Johnny cleared his throat and smiled. "Hello, everyone, I'm Johnny Briggs. I'm here to emphasize the importance of quality illustration in your published works."

Paul scanned the room. The audience was attentive, leaning forward in their seats. Their eyes flitted from Johnny to the projector and back. Paul sighed.

Johnny knew how to engage a crowd. They didn't realize he had no vision. The guy was a rip-off artist —he'd stolen his creative processes from Paul. Right down to the brand of pencils and graphics program. And his art was all derivative—offshoots of others' successes.

Johnny walked to the front of the stage, waving a hand over the audience. "Everyone knows the saying 'don't judge a book by its cover', right?" He nodded emphatically, and the crowd joined him.

Paul didn't nod.

"Raise your hand if you've heard that before!" He raised a hand, and the audience raised theirs. He thanked them silently with his lips, and they let their arms fall back to their laps. "But I think we all know that readers do exactly that. Am I right?"

The crowd was all nods and murmurs, turning to one another and smiling.

"But that's still not good enough, folks."

The crowd grew quiet with anticipation. Paul scowled.

It was infuriating how Johnny's thievery *worked*. Paul's greatest professional regret was going into business with him after they graduated from New Brimswick's Art Academy. The partnership hadn't lasted long—six months of Johnny stealing Paul's ideas and creative processes while polishing his marketing prowess. After their split, the market hadn't rewarded Paul's greater intrinsic skill. Instead, Johnny's career had flourished because he was an absolute star at selling his work. And here, displayed on expensive conference equipment, his "art" looked better than it deserved.

"You can have a nice cover for your magazine," Johnny continued. "You can have a solid illustration inside your beloved novel. It might have cost a pretty penny too. And it all might still not be *good enough*."

Johnny pointed backward at his projected illustrations, keeping his attention on the crowd. "You need the very *best*."

Paul kicked himself for not checking the speaker listing before attending this session. If he'd known his nemesis was presenting, he would have opted for a different session. And if he left now, Johnny would see him.

*The bastard would get amusement from that. He'd consider it professional jealousy.*

Paul chose to ignore his presentation instead. He'd focus on developing his strategy for the rest of the conference. Bills were piling up—he needed to get better at this networking thing. He needed to *sell work*.

"Take a look!" Johnny's boisterous voice pulled Paul's attention to the stage. "Time for a critical lesson. Let's compare."

Johnny waved to a stagehand and a second, older

projector lit up. The screen was much duller than the one featuring Johnny's drawings. The hazy images lacked crisp lines and the tonal balance was off. The illustrations looked bland, washed up.

"There are good illustrations here. But how do these look to you, folks?" Johnny scrunched his face and shrugged his shoulders. He raised one hand and turned it quickly from side to side in a *so-so* gesture. "I'd put these in the *not good enough* bucket, wouldn't you?"

Paul barely heard the last words. One illustration had captured his gaze, locking it in place. It was *Madeline*, the green-scaled lady with serpentine features and long red nails. It was one of Paul's greatest works, but here it looked terrible—her pale skin unimpressive, her normally striking eyes, dull. Her shape was ill-defined in the projector's poor contrast, blending into the background cavern.

"Poor sales will result," Johnny continued. "Those are the facts."

Blood rushed to Paul's face. He clenched a fist. His lips curled back into a snarl.

*That bastard!*

Further down on the screen, his eyes found another of his illustrations—*The Great Tree*. The poor display masked its intricacies. The detail of the leaves and the latticework of imagery within the many branches. All lost. The trunk was a hideous mustard-seed color. Bland, uninspiring, ugly.

This was a first. He'd never seen Johnny show his work in a demeaning light. Copying was one thing—this was a whole new level. He wanted to scream. To call Johnny out on the whole thing. But that would appear unhinged. His rival would spin it until he was the victim. No—he wouldn't give him that opportunity. He'd confront him at the end. Paul closed his eyes and took a deep breath.

"Well, that's it for today, folks." Johnny's full voice echoed across the room. "I hope you learned something useful. If you'd like to talk with me after the presentation, I'll be here until late tonight and all day tomorrow. I'd love to help you propel your projects to success."

The audience applauded, then stood and filtered into the exhibition halls leaving Johnny behind in the suite, packing his duffel bag with his portfolio and tech equipment.

"Hey! What do you think you're doing?!" Paul's voice was loud on his approach.

Johnny turned toward him and nodded in recognition before standing. "Hey, Paul. Did you like the presentation? Good conference so far."

Paul pointed at him. "You need to take my work out of your scam-of-a-presentation right now."

Johnny held his hands out in reconciliation.

"Whoa, okay. Lighten up, big guy. I thought you'd like the free publicity. After all, obscurity is the greatest threat to our livelihoods. I'm not sure anyone knows who you are. I've been making a killing since our split, but you … not so well, am I right?"

"Don't act like you're trying to help. You're making me look bad with your sleazy tactics."

"Hey, no problem, Pauly. If you're that gun-shy, I'll take them down. But, you should expect that I'd highlight *my* art in *my* seminar. Isn't that what any businessman with a brain would do? You could do your own presentation too, you know. But that's your problem, Paul. You just want to doodle. Sad, because I think you have the potential for more."

"Just take my work out of your presentation or you'll be getting a call from my attorney."

Footsteps approached from behind, followed by a deep, nasally voice. "I'm sorry to interrupt, but are you Paul Desmontes?"

Paul turned to see a short balding man, round of head, with weasel eyes and a beak-like nose. He wore a dapper suit of black and lavender with silver buttons and carried a dueling cane. Paul recognized the man. It was Clive Murkin, Head of the *Elite Illustration Society*—a network of prestigious illustrators dubbed The Society for short. His group had secured several lucrative contracts in recent years. Paul hadn't ever seen Clive—or any representative from their group—in person. He didn't think they were from the area. But The Society was well known, and Clive's photo had been on several high-end advertisements.

"Yes, I'm Paul."

Clive held out a hand, and Paul shook it. "I saw your name on the attendee list. I've been meaning to speak with you, Paul. We've had our eye on you for some time. The Elite Illustration Society has an opening. Are you free to talk for a few minutes?"

"Sure." Something about Clive seemed off, and Paul had reservations about The Society. Their artists all adopted a similar, comic style that didn't appeal to him—and each was so similar that it became difficult to tell them apart. He preferred a more gritty, realistic approach. And he liked to do things his own way. However, The Society was commercially successful, and he needed money. It couldn't hurt to talk.

Clive winked and gestured to the door. "Perfect. Let's go chat at my vendor table."

On the way out, Paul glanced back at Johnny. The bravado had fled his rival's face, replaced by scarlet skin and narrow, jealous eyes.

Paul smiled. Maybe something was finally going his way.

# CHAPTER TWO

PAUL STOOD beside Clive Murkin at The Elite Illustration Society's vendor table, trying his best not to tower over the penguin-like man.

Clive flipped through The Society's portfolio, finger sliding over the artist bios. "As Head of The Society, I've played a key role in recruitment. Sam Hawkins, Priscilla Scrimp, Rufio Fortezzo … could you ask for better company, Mr. Desmontes?"

"Good company indeed, Mr. Murkin."

Paul recognized each one. All respected industry names. Genuine artists who had rendered iconic imagery across graphic novels, comics, and movie advertisements. The elegance of Fortezzo's *Amazon Woman* had yet to be eclipsed, despite being a decade old. No one could claim a sharper, more daring contrast than Scrimp's interpretation of the *Creature from the Black Lagoon*. There were no hacks here. No two-bit scum sketchers like Johnny Briggs. It would make perfect business sense to join such elite company. It would be an honor, except ...

"Please ... call me Clive." He tapped his cane on the tile floor.

Paul nodded. "The Society has amassed a truly impressive organization of artists, Clive. Each has produced awe-inspiring work, and deserves my respect."

Clive stood taller, turning toward him. "Why do I sense an impending 'but'?"

"Well," Paul waved a hand over the portfolio. "These illustrations are all from the artists' early days ... before they joined The Elite Illustration Society, correct?"

The Head nodded. "Very perceptive, Paul." His voice was as coaxing and warm as a deep, nasally voice could hope to be. "We haven't gotten to the modern depictions yet. Look here." He flipped a few more pages, past a separator clearly denoted "Works of The Elite Illustration Society."

Paul frowned.

*Would they own all of my drawings? Not sure how I feel about that...*

Paul recognized many of the images that followed, all professional and refined, with similar curvature in the pencil strokes, the playful lines embracing a comic feel. The art was all impressive, but it was stylistically redundant—whether Scrimps, Hawkins, or another. The same artist might have created all of them.

*If my own work is to be a simple clone of this style, why hire me?*

"These look great." Paul couldn't hide his diluted tone.

"I hear hesitation in your voice." Clive closed the book and placed a hand on Paul's sleeve. "Don't you see? We think your art is inspired. You belong with us. That's not something to take lightly." His beak-like nose drifted downward beneath an accusatory stare.

Paul shrunk slowly back from the light touch. "I'm honored, Clive. I just need a little time to consider. If I joined, would all future work belong to The Society?"

Clive nodded. "When you're in, you're in. However, you will have steady, gainful employment. And The Society's contracts are growing *exponentially*. You could say goodbye to freelance dime-work."

*No more starving artist.*

Paul bit down on his lip. Despite his reservations, the pitch sounded enticing. Bills were piling up. But why had they waited so long to reach out to him? The Elite Illustration Society had been around for years. And why had they never been at any other local events?

"You said there was a new opening—did someone leave the group?"

A look of displeasure seemed to flash across Clive's face, though Paul couldn't be sure. "Circumstances required one to retire." He shrugged. "It is no matter. A door closed for one, and it opened for another. So, what do you say? I have an assignment ready upon your acceptance."

"Let me sleep on it, Clive. I'm honored, but it's a big decision." He nodded and sauntered around the table. The hallway was mostly clear now, the conference attendees having rushed to their next sessions.

Clive extended a business card across the table, tapping his cane on the floor as Paul took the card. "Call me. The door closes in three days."

# CHAPTER
# THREE

PAUL'S FACE grew hotter with each envelope he shredded. His mood always took a dive when reviewing bills. He glared up at the clock, its face fashioned after the infamous vampire, Nosferatu. It seemed to watch him with amusement.

"Public utilities—two months behind? No. I made a half payment last month. The water smells like bad eggs, anyway."

He ripped in half a solicitation for insect control. He tore another—an ad aimed at marketing his illustration business, *Desmontes Touch*. Several minutes later, his hand rested on the final envelope. He looked at his fingernails, bitten down to the skin. This last bill was the eye of his financial maelstrom—his loan with Gracious Heart Lending.

A year ago, he'd used the equity in his house to

take a gamble at expanding his business. His illustrations were receiving stellar reviews, but he needed larger clientele. So, he'd poured money into advertising. He'd networked with contacts in big cities to expand his distribution beyond nearby New Brimswick. All had failed. Business never picked up. His contacts had turned out to be incompetent, more likely disingenuous, in their efforts. That would have been bad enough, but he had made a critical mistake next, thinking he just needed more grease on the wheels to get his business rolling. He had doubled down on his spend, depleting his equity. Nothing meaningful changed in the end, aside from new, overwhelming debt. He had picked up a few clients, but not enough to even cover his loan payments.

Paul clenched his teeth as he ripped open the Gracious Heart envelope. "Dear Mr. Desmontes," he read aloud in a mocking voice. He didn't bother with the rest. Instead, taking a deep breath, he walked over to the hearth, where the fire crackled and swayed. He grabbed the tongs and placed the bill in their grip, bringing the paper slowly to the flame, watching the words burn in a cathartic haze. He pumped air with the bellows, watching the flames grow until the final shreds of the bill disappeared.

Afterward, he poured himself gin at the bar, smiling grimly. He would allow himself this moment. Reality could wait. His gaze fell upon his father's photograph over the mantle. The two had loved each other, but his father never understood Paul's art, expecting Paul to follow him into the mines as he had followed his own father. Paul's father had died from the black lung at forty-six, when Paul was still a young man.

Paul had nearly succumbed to his father's expectations. He'd worked in the coal mines for several years before giving his illustration business a chance. He had made a modest living at it, too, until his financial blunders derailed him.

He turned to Nosferatu. "Is it over, old friend? Is it my time to die in the mines?"

The clock struck nine and Nosferatu grinned, his eyes glowing their nightly devilish red. For the third time that evening, Paul pulled up the business card from the counter and inspected it—*Clive Murkin – Head of the Elite Illustration Society.*

He sighed and pulled out his portfolio, containing a copy of every illustration he had ever done. He flipped through his renditions of the *Hounds of the Baskerville* and *Sirens of the Deep*. The *Poltergeist* seemed to return his gaze through an ethereal membrane.

He could remember the exact moment in time he had crafted each one. Their reception had been limited, but warm. Each clearly encompassed the *Desmontes Touch*. His style was his own. Even the mines couldn't take that from him. But The Elite Illustration Society could. They could water his art down and gut him. But was selling out truly worse than the mines?

"That, my dear boy, is the question of the night," he said to himself, downing another glass of gin.

Those seemed his only options ... he knew nothing else. The truth of the matter was that The Society's illustrations weren't bad. They sold for a reason, after all. He didn't *hate* them, but the work was repetitive and lacked soul. Why hire a unique talent if they wanted duplication? The act of creation only made Paul feel alive when it was *his own*. If he wanted a complacent life—or one of following others' orders—he would have stayed in the mines.

Paul could, however, continue to do his sketches on the side, in his own style. He could just save them until he was no longer contracted with The Elite Illustration Society. This would allow him to pay the bills, while satisfying his true artistic expression. When he finally broke free from The Society, he'd have an entire new portfolio to market! And they wouldn't own the work if they didn't know about it ...

Paul grabbed his cell phone from the bar and walked to the kitchen. He dialed the number from the business card.

"This is Clive," came the nasally voice.

"Hi. It's Paul Desmontes. I've given your offer some consideration."

"Excellent. So, are you in? Your offer is a full 15% bump over our last recruit. Keep that confidential, please."

"I want to go over the paperwork ... but yes, I'm in."

"Of course. A package will arrive at your door tonight. It will have the contract, as well as an important piece of jewelry."

Paul shook his head, hoping to break his brain free from the liquor. "Umm ... did you say jewelry, Mr. Murkin?"

Clive's laugh reminded Paul of a weasel. "It's nothing fancy. A pin from The Society, as a welcome."

Paul laughed, relieved. "A pin? Okay, thanks."

"If the contract is to your liking, you will receive a check one week from today. It will include a six-month advance. As long as you are on task with assignments, of course. The amounts are detailed in the contract. We like to extend our new recruits a warm welcome."

Paul's eyes widened. "Six months' pay? Wow ... thank you. I uh—"

"Now, a couple of things. As a member of the Elite Illustration Society, you will always wear your pin. You may take it off to bathe, to sleep, of course. Otherwise, you wear it. It's free advertisement for

The Society, and a source of pride while you sketch. It's a beautiful piece of jewelry that shall adorn you. Got it? It's in your contract. Don't let any of us catch you pinless."

*That's a lot of to-do over a pin …*

"Item number two is your assignment. You will sketch the Wolfman. Start by looking at historical interpretations. Then, make it your own while merging it with company branding. You'll see detailed, illustrated instruction in the packet containing your contract. That's it. Welcome to The Society, Paul."

Paul scratched his cheek, unsure of what to say. "The Wolfman. Got it. I'll work on it."

"Good. We'll talk again in a few days to gauge progress."

The line went dead.

Paul held the phone out, dumbfounded, before setting it on the kitchen counter.

*Six months' pay for one drawing. Six months' pay!*

An hour later, there was a knock at his door. When he opened it, no one was there, but a package lay at his feet. Inside was a lengthy contract and a small jewelry box containing a shiny, black pin with E.I.S. in gold lettering. On the back, engraved in the tiniest of lowercase letters, read *paul desmontes*.

# CHAPTER
# FOUR

PAUL TAPPED a finger on his desk, satisfied. He had spent the day researching, starting at the library and finishing with an internet search at home. There had been six primary depictions of the Wolfman going all the way back to the 1300s. As expected, the biggest shifts had happened from one century to the next, with intermittent iterations closely mirroring one another. The original resembled a man with wolfish features; Dark, thick hair, like fur, and an extended jaw. Throughout the years, the interpretation became more beast than man—jaw protruding further, teeth growing, hair thickening, stance lowering.

In the first six pages of a new sketchbook, he had recreated the primary depictions in his own realistic, noir style. The original Wolfman was his favorite, an ink illustration by Miles Studenberg. You could almost mistake the creature for a man in the interpretation. The eyes held a feeble sadness, at odds with the intimidating physique. Later depictions harmonized this dissonance, replacing the disquieting gaze with one of wild rage. During his research, Paul had found a book titled *The Myth of the Wolfman*, the creature's origin story. The description suggested the Wolfman had been a normal man who suffered from an unsightly genetic condition. Society had shunned him and he had lived in isolation in the woods, surviving alongside wolves for a time. The story sounded interesting—Paul would have to read it after this project was complete.

A gust of wind pressed against the office window, remnants of the chill air somehow gaining entrance and seeping through holes in his sweater. He rubbed his hands together and stood to stretch. He left for the fireplace, which he suspected might need tending.

*The first paycheck alone will make this contract worthwhile. I might actually afford to use the furnace to heat this place.*

In the living room, a healthy fire still burned. It just wasn't pumping enough heat to offset the frigid northeast winter. The Nosferatu clock watched him closely from the kitchen, and Paul returned its gaze. "No. I will not turn the heat on. Do you think me weak?" Paul grabbed a second shirt from his bedroom and put it on beneath his sweater before returning to his office. Back in his chair, he glanced through the depictions again, tracing his finger over each one until he reached the blank page where he would create his own sketch.

All day, he had worn the black pin he received in the mail, feeling its tiny metal backing poke his chest like an accusatory finger. The prodding continued, even with another shirt. It was downright odd. With each breath, the pin seemed to etch itself into his chest. It was more uncomfortable than painful. Still—he wanted to take the thing off. But he remembered Clive's words: "It's in your contract. Don't let any of us catch you pinless."

But how would they know if he took it off? He clutched the pin, but hesitated, thinking of his Nosferatu clock. If it were in this room, its head would be shaking in disapproval, if such a thing were possible. The antique kept him in line, though he hated it at times. He would wear the pin for now. He stretched his sweater away from his chest for a moment to relieve the pressure. It was just a little poking, after all.

Paul sketched an outline of the Wolfman's head with a light charcoal pencil. His interpretation would attempt to bring the original's humanity back into the illustration. He might do that while keeping to

The Society's required pastiche. Beside his sketchbook, his contract lay open to a page with several detailed examples. The style, polished and whimsical, was not to his tastes. The Wolfman would look like a caricature without the exaggerated features—a comic portrayal. Not the three-dimensional, gritty depiction he would prefer—a man with undertones of monster and melancholy.

He sketched the creature's head, his arm sweeping with ease, as if pulled by invisible strings. He bore down on the pencil point with precision, outlining and shading gracefully. Moments later, he finished the first pass. He didn't care for it, but it closely matched The Society's prescribed style. The illustration should please Clive. And the creature's intelligent eyes mirrored the original depiction. That was a win, at least.

He couldn't have been illustrating for more than a few minutes when a cold weariness seeped into his flesh. The pin dug into his chest like a finch's beak. Paul winced and pulled at his sweater again.

*Curse this thing.*

Paul stood and stretched, yawning. In the kitchen, he boiled water and made hazelberry tea, pouring it into his ceramic Wendigo mug. Its antelope skull protruded from the front—allowing room enough to sip—and antlers rose high from the sides. It was one of his favorite cryptids, the lore so close to home. He glanced out the window to the thick woods beyond the clearing of his backyard. The steam from his mug warmed his face, and he sipped, careful not to burn his lips.

He opened his refrigerator, taking inventory—one egg, no milk, meatloaf, and half a stick of butter, along with some leftovers. A trip to the grocery store was in order. First, though, he would look through the historical depictions again. He could kick them around in his head, all the better prepared when he returned. Back at his desk, he flipped back through the pages while the hot tea slid down his throat, and he acknowledged each interpretation, going backward through time. When he got to the original, he paused, his eyes narrowing. He scratched his head. Something about it seemed different.

*Did it ... change?*

The Wolfman held the same position, standing amongst the trees at the edge of a forest, staring out into a clearing. But it seemed a little closer, and where before the eyes had held a deep sadness, now rage consumed them. A chill spread through Paul's bones, and the pin dug like a dagger tip into his chest. He closed the sketchbook and pulled at his sweater.

This couldn't be right. He must have gotten the illustrations mixed up somehow. No big deal.

*I just need some fresh air. I'll feel better by the time I return.*

Paul finished his hazelberry tea and got to his feet. On the way to the front door, he could feel Nosferatu's glare at his back. The vampire itched for his attention, but Paul didn't turn back. Instead, he threw on his boots and down jacket, grabbed his keys, and left the house.

# CHAPTER
# FIVE

PAUL DROVE his Subaru wagon toward Rahl's Food Market. The icy, winding roads made him think of the curving lines of the Wolfman's jaw, spine, and legs. The needles from the fir trees on either side gave the illusion of the creature's fur. A feeling spread from his gut, urging him to turn around and get back to task. He should be completing his illustration, not dawdling around town for milk and eggs. But what was wrong with taking a break?

The pin stuck in his chest like the tip of a freshly sharpened paring knife. "Aagh!" He unzipped his jacket and pulled at his sweater to relieve the pressure. He longed to pull it off, but again hesitated. Freezing wind snuck through the crack in the rear left window of his car—which wouldn't roll all the way up—finding the access of his open jacket, and chilling his skin. He shivered, gripping the steering wheel tighter.

Several minutes later, he pulled into the parking lot at Rahl's, which was near capacity. Many came from the nearby city of New Brimswick to the South. He opened the car door, zipped his jacket, and placed one foot on the asphalt before stopping, remembering Clive's words. *"Don't let us catch you pinless. It's free advertising for The Society."* The pin wasn't visible now, he realized. He unzipped his jacket and wrestled it free from his sweater, feeling immediate relief.

He inspected the pin under the winter sun. The gold letters "E.I.S." stood raised over the black plating. The backing held his name, scrawled in lower case cursive. He didn't want to wear it again. Yet, he found himself zipping his jacket and fastening the pin on the front. It clasped easily into its backing despite the jacket's thickness, as if the stem had lengthened to accommodate.

*At least now I won't feel it poking me.*

Paul crossed the lot toward the store. From nearby pine trees, loose needles rained onto the pavement, whisked along by the wind. A middle-aged woman wearing a Russian ear-flap hat escorted two young boys to her SUV. The children shielded their faces from the icy winds and nestled beneath her thick coat like penguins. A man in butchers overalls and big black boots carried a giant paper bag, likely filled with red meat. The wind wrestled his thick mustache away from his cheeks in wild bursts. He steeled a glance at Paul, holding the gaze a sliver too long for comfort.

Inside, lines stretched into the aisles from all twelve bagging lanes. A toy train chugged along a track suspended from the ceiling rafters, tooting its horn every few seconds. Paul navigated the crowds to get the few items he needed. Along the way, he passed—with great hunger lust—fresh porterhouse steaks and Lithuanian sausages. He passed blueberry pies and dragon fruit and coconut crumpets. He didn't have Nosferatu here to keep him in line, but he somehow refrained from carting anything he didn't need. Those items were not in his budget.

*Not* yet *at least ...*

In the check-out line, he felt an irritation—a tiny, barely discernible prodding like a sharp-footed insect tapping on his chest. He looked down, and his mouth fell open a little.

*The pin again?!*

He could feel it through his jacket and sweater and the two underlying shirts. The irritation grew to the jab of a spruce needle, and he pulled at his jacket to relieve the poking.

When he looked up again, he caught, in an adjacent line, the gaze of an older woman, weathered but well-kempt, perhaps in her sixties. Long, wavy black and grey hair draped around an almond-shaped face of earthy beauty. Fierce green eyes blazed like a jade fire, locking him in place until it seemed to be just the two of them. Her eyes shifted downward to his jacket. A man behind Paul cleared his throat, and Paul broke eye contact with the woman. The line had moved up, and now he shuffled his cart forward. The woman was no longer in view, hidden behind the register shelves.

Paul sighed with relief when the total at checkout was within his means. Afterward, he skittered across the sleet to his station wagon and began to load his groceries.

The wind carried a woman's apprehensive voice to his ear. "W–where did you get that pin?"

It was the green-eyed lady from the line. She held her hair like a scarf against her neck. With the other hand, she pointed to the pin on Paul's jacket. Her gaze fell intently on the object. The sides of her mouth drooped and quivered. The shine he had seen in her eyes, no longer there.

"I've seen you here before, but never with that pin," she said.

Paul frowned. "I got it recently. It represents The Elite Illustration Socie—"

"I know what it is." Her gaze lifted to meet his. "You should get rid of it. Who are you?"

Paul took a quick breath, and the chilly wind forced a shiver. The pin poked at his chest, reminding him he had an illustration to get back to. "I'm Paul. Look, I'm not sure what this is all about, but it's just a pin. No big deal."

The woman took a step closer. "My name is Serafina. My brother, Nigel, was in The Society. I visited him shortly after he joined." She stared at him with vacant eyes now. Her voice softened and her words slowed to a crawl. "He looked terrible—dark circles under his eyes, skeleton-thin. He started acting insane. Forgetting things."

"Look—I'm terribly sorry about your brother, but it's cold out here and—"

"Listen!" Serafina stepped close enough for her frosted breath to mix with his own. "He said his drawings were changing somehow. He said they *moved*."

Paul froze, thinking of his first illustration of the Wolfman, how the eyes seemed to have changed.

*Impossible. This is all just a coincidence.*

"It sounds like your brother might need some help," he said.

"Maybe I could have done something, but he asked me to leave," she muttered. "He said he was too busy for visitors."

Paul started to turn away, but the woman would not let him break her gaze.

"Two days later, he was found dead in his apartment. The police did not report a cause. They investigated, but nothing came of it. I drove to his place many times to get answers, but they wouldn't let me in."

"Why are you telling me all this?"

"Because," she continued. "I saw someone from The Elite Illustration Society talking with the investigator more than once. A short, bald man named Clive. Soon after, a fire spread throughout Nigel's building, destroying any evidence of what happened. But I know it was them, Paul. Somehow. It was The Society."

The pin placed steady pressure on Paul's chest now.

"The last time I saw Nigel before he died, he wore that pin," Serafina whispered. She pointed at it, her eyes wild. "He never took it off. Is that the same one … pulled from my brother's corpse?"

That was too much. Heart racing, Paul slammed the trunk and scrambled to the driver's seat. He pulled the door shut behind him, pretending the woman was not there. He sat, breathing heavily, skin crawling, feeling just as cold inside the car as he had outside of it. When he turned his head, Serafina's breath frosted against his window. Her feral gaze was upon him. She tapped three times.

Paul frantically started the car and cracked the window as little as possible. "I have to go."

But Serafina's words slithered like pit vipers to his ear. "I saw one of Nigel's drawings. Tell me you're not doing the same ones, Paul. Tell me you're not drawing the Wolfman."

# CHAPTER SIX

PAUL DROVE HOME IN SHOCK. He'd left his house to clear his mind, but his trip to Rahl's had had the opposite effect. Clearly, Serafina was unhinged. Probably an independent artist that lost business to The Society. One crazy enough to think up an elaborate story of murder and obstruction of justice. But there was one thing bothering him about his theory.

*The Wolfman. How could she know my assignment?*

He arrived back home to find a red car parked in front of his house. Curious, he brought his groceries to the front door and then walked to the side of the Audi, squinting to see inside. Johnny Briggs sat in the driver's seat, and Paul's day grew immediately worse. Johnny rolled down his window and leaned over.

"Hey, man! Like my new ride? I was in the neighborhood. Thought I'd stop by to see an old friend."

"We're not friends, Johnny. The worst thing I ever did was go into business with you. What do you want?" The pin prodded his chest like a hungry kitten's claw.

Johnny laughed and smoothed the collar of his sports coat. "Come now, Paul. We've had our differences, but let's leave the past behind. You'll be happy to know I've updated my display to remove your art. Speaking of presentations, I'm giving one this coming weekend at New Brimswick's General Arts Festival. Tickets are selling fast, so you should get yours soon."

"I'm still wondering what you want." Paul crossed his arms.

Johnny tapped the steering wheel, smiling wickedly. He leaned in closer. "Okay, okay. I just came here to let you know … we're brothers now."

"Enough with the games, Johnny. I've got work to do."

Johnny flashed his white teeth. "The Illustration Society reached out to me after the conference. It turns out they want me in their club, after all. I look forward to seeing you at more events."

Paul frowned. That made little sense. Why would they ignore Johnny at the conference, only to call him later? His eyes narrowed as he scanned his rival's black sports coat. No pin.

*Aha! He's lying.*

"Aren't you missing something?" Paul asked, smirking.

The cocky smile evaporated from Johnny's face. "What?"

"If you were in The Society, you'd have your honorary pin." He tapped his own.

"Oh … right. It's in the mail. I should get it today." His face reddened.

*Sure it is.*

"Well, nice of you to stop by, Johnny. Let's catch up later."

"Let's do that. Don't forget to get your ticket for this weekend. I might be able to reserve you a front-row seat for my presentation!" He rolled up his window and sped off, tires squealing.

Paul fanned exhaust from his face as Johnny disappeared around a bend in the road.

*Imagine being so jealous that you stalk your competition, show up at their house to gloat, and lie to them about being a part of an organization.*

Paul grabbed his groceries from the front step and went inside the house. It was time to resume his illustration.

# CHAPTER SEVEN

PAUL'S WRIST hovered over the sketchpad as if suspended from tiny puppet strings. It swept from side to side as he illustrated the hunching shoulders and hulking torso of the wolfman in The Society's style. His entire body seemed to move along with the motion of his wrists, as if swaying in an ocean current. He paused twice, pulling his sweater at the site of the pin.

He was sketching the creature's thighs when his cell rang, disturbing his task like harsh sunlight invading a dream. He stood and stretched, feeling like he woke for the first time that day, and accepted the call.

"Hello, Paul." Clive's voice seeped like sludge. "How is the Wolfman?"

"He's coming along. I'm more than halfway

done." Something about Paul's new employer made him anxious. He walked into the kitchen, holding the phone to his ear.

"I want you to own the process, Paul. Put all of yourself into it."

"Of course, Mr. Murkin. I expect to be finished with the draft tonight."

Clive breathed into the phone for several seconds before speaking again. "Good ... good. And how are you *feeling* about it?"

Paul tugged at his pin, which scraped like a thorn at his chest. "Great. Everything is ... going well."

Feeling Nosferatu's gaze, he glanced up at the clock. *No mention of the harassing pin, or your troubling encounters? No mention of how your drawing changed?* the vampire seemed to say.

Paul clenched a fist. He wanted to rip Nosferatu from the wall and stomp on his smirking face. Paul's blood-sucking companion seemed to turn against him more each day. But the vampire made good points. He always did.

"There *is* one thing..." Paul said into the phone. "Did you offer Johnny Briggs employment? I ran into him, and he said he's part of The Society now."

Clive laughed. "No. He's a showman, not an artist. He charms others into believing the opposite, but it doesn't work on us, Paul."

*Unbelievable. Johnny is a loose cannon.*

"Besides. If he was one of us," Clive continued, "you would have seen his pin. You *are* wearing yours, right?"

Paul was acutely aware of the thing poking him like an ice pick. "Yes."

"Good. I look forward to the final illustration later today." The line went dead.

Paul stared at the phone for a few seconds before heading back to his desk. There seemed no transition period between sitting and resuming his sketch. Instead, his arm rose on its own and his wrist floated like a phantom. He delicately stroked the pencil's point across the page for the Wolfman's finer details, and he leaned in with intent to create muscle and sinew. Paul was minutely aware, somewhere in the back of his mind, of his general displeasure with the caricaturistic style he was imposing upon the page. But at the same time, it felt just right. After a while, he finished the Wolfman, aside from final shading and detail.

The pencil fell from his hand as if on its own. Paul rose, stretching. He realized the pin's incessant prodding had ceased. He had been experiencing a surplus of anxiety over this entire ordeal. His new employment and the prospect of selling out had sliced like a scythe clean into his psyche, inducing paranoia. He looked down at the pin. How could a tiny piece of metal torment him? No, he realized now that the suffering had been self-imposed. His own delusion, yet he warmed to the notion as he leaned forward and slid a loving fingertip over the length of his illustration, meeting the beast's gaze.

*Nearly finished. Time for a quick bite and some tea.*

Paul brought his empty Wendigo mug to the kitchen and set it on the counter. He boiled some water for his tea and grabbed last night's leftover pork chops and yams from the fridge, heating them in a pan. The meat was a cheap cut, tough and gristly, but he had learned over time how skillful seasoning could mask inferior quality. When the food was ready, he took a bite. The flavor was satisfying, but chewing was tough and it left his jaw muscles sore.

*Haven't quite figured out the texture issue. Oh well, soon enough I may afford a better meal.*

A moment later, he poured fresh tea into his mug and glanced up at the clock. Nosferatu looked at him with wonder, as if to say, *So that's it? All is well now, Paul?* If the vampire could shake his head and smirk, he would. But it was just an inanimate object, and Paul ignored it. The vampire was like a depressed family member. One that was not real.

*I think it's time for a new clock. Soon as I get paid...*

Outside, fresh snow fell. At the hearth, the fire had diminished to glowing embers. He set his meal aside and walked over to stoke the flame, adding kindling and a log, watching it blaze anew.

A loud crash from the other room nearly sent him tumbling into the fireplace. The poker slipped from his grasp and he stiffened, his heart jumping to his throat. He ran toward the sound. When he reached the office, his jaw fell open. The pin stuck in him like a nail before a stern hammering. Shattered glass lay across the floor and freezing wind blasted inward, drawing toward him with its icy embrace.

There was no sign of an intruder, but someone had smashed one of his office windows from the outside. When Paul glanced at his sketchbook, still open where he had left it, panic seized him. He hunched over in disbelief, catching himself with one hand on his desk.

The page containing his illustration was gone. Fragments of paper at the binding revealed it had been torn out.

Breathing deeply the frigid night air, a conclusion lodged like an anchor into his brain.

*Johnny Briggs!*

Who else could it have been? Professional jealousy was a powerful motivator. Ignoring the open window, Paul ran to the front of the house, where he threw on his jacket, boots, and hat. He ignored Nosferatu's questioning glance on his way. He burst out of the front door, eyes blazing, head on a swivel, looking for his rival's car.

But the street was empty. Paul took another deep breath, watching the cold air rush like smoke.

*He must have sped off in his quiet new ride. Well, I know where you live, Johnny. Did you think I'd just let this slide??*

He ran back inside, snatched his keys from the hook, and drove off in his station wagon.

## CHAPTER
# EIGHT

IT TOOK Paul nearly half an hour to reach Johnny's house. He'd sped the entire way, eyes peeled for the enemy between each falling snowflake, around each winding bend of the road. But he hadn't seen him. Now, parked a quarter block shy of Johnny's house, Paul crept along the trees which bordered the spacious lots of the upscale suburban neighborhood. He wanted the element of surprise.

*But to what end?*

Paul realized he had no actual plan. He only knew that Johnny had broken his window and stolen his art. His blood boiled intensely, like it could spill right out of his ears to the snow. And since the incident, he was noticing the pin again—a focused pressure point on his chest now, as if pinning him like an insect to a spreading board.

The wide-open front lawn would leave him exposed, so he crept toward the house along the side nearest him, pausing before the light from a large first-floor window could catch him. Staying close to the house, he sidled toward the light until a TV screen came into view through the window. He crouched and leaned forward, revealing an arm resting on the edge of a couch ...

Paul flinched. His eyes bulged.

*Impossible.*

Johnny Briggs was watching TV with his arm around his wife, Eleanor. A basket of popcorn sat between them. Their son lay on a fake bearskin rug facing the screen. The way they were settled in, he would guess they had been there at least 10 or 15 minutes—probably more. Paul had sped here straight away—there would be no time for Johnny to have all this set up.

*But if he's not the perpetrator ... then who?*

Eleanor turned in Paul's direction and seemed to lean a bit toward the window, narrowing her eyes.

Paul lowered himself slowly and crept backward until he was out of view. He retreated, avoiding the lights wherever possible. Inside his car, his chest throbbed at the point of the pin. He whipped off his jacket and pulled his sweater's collar outward, staring down at his chest. He expected to see an inflamed mark where it had been inflicting its damage. But there was no wound or sign of irritation at all.

*Impossible.*

He swabbed his chest with two fingers, bringing his hand up and inspecting it under his car's interior light. No blood.

*If Johnny didn't smash my window, and this pin's not doing anything to me ... could this all be some sort of hallucination?*

But someone had shattered his window. That was real. He had seen the glass shards on his office floor. He had felt the freezing wind inside the house. His sketchbook was missing the page with his illustration. Then there was that business with that woman, Serafina, at the grocery store. Clearly, she was unstable.

*Or was she?*

Paul drove back home, one hand clenching at the hair atop his head, squeezing and feeling the strain on his scalp. Occasionally, he ran a fingertip over the pin fastened to his sweater and thought of Clive Murkin. His employer would expect a draft of the Wolfman tonight.

*I'm done. Forget The Society. And forget this pin!*

Paul gripped the pin in his hand and meant to rip it off, but something tore the desire from his head.

He arrived home to an icebox. Wind howled

through the broken window. In the living room, the fire had died, choked out by the frigid air, and a chill enveloped his body—the heat from his earlier rage gone. He stepped out to the backyard with a flashlight to inspect the site around the window for clues of the perpetrator. Nothing was there. The dense, dark woods less than eight yards from the back of his house seemed to inch closer as he grabbed a sheet of plywood and duct tape from his shed. Back inside, he covered the broken window with the plywood, pushing against the wind, and running tape along the edges to secure it. While not a perfect fit, it would work for now.

He peered through the unbroken window on the lefthand side into darkness. A blast of wind pulled his attention back to his right, where the duct tape was visibly straining. Paul ran outside and leaned more plywood against the broken window as a buffer. The woods seemed to creep closer as he returned to the house, glancing back over his shoulder to the wilderness. Inside, he locked the door and lit the fireplace, adding kindling and wood. After a few minutes, the blaze had grown enough for him to remove his hat. Several minutes later, he pulled off his down jacket.

Behind Paul, Nosferatu's inquisitive glare penetrated the back of his skull. He turned to the clock, his heart rising into his throat.

*Who broke the window, Paul?* Nosferatu seemed to say.

"I don't know. So just *shut up* for now," Paul seethed.

Paul knew if it could, the vampire would be sighing at his ignorance.

The pin jabbed like an accusatory finger, reminding him of his task. Why hadn't he just pulled the damned thing off?? He should have thrown it into the fire long ago. Maybe he couldn't take it off at all.

*But I took it off before. At the grocery store.*

Nosferatu seemed to shake his head. *You took it off, intending to put it right back on. That's like not taking it off at all.*

"I told you to be silent," Paul snapped, pointing at the clock.

He ran into the office and sat at his desk, where his sketchbook was still at the torn page. He pulled off the remaining bits of paper at the binding and threw them over his shoulder in disgust. Pencil in hand, he began to recreate the Wolfman. His memory held the stolen illustration, and he stroked the pad with determination, making steady progress. His wrist again hovered over the pad as if guided by a puppet master, bearing down for emphasis at the beast's hide and claws and lifting at each stroke's edge. After a while, he paused, remembering something. He had wanted to bring humanity into the beast's eyes. Like Miles Studenberg had done in the first illustration.

Paul flipped back to the original drawing for inspiration and froze. His lips trembled.

The Wolfman looked different. Its head was turned in his direction now, and it seemed to stare at him. On the ground, scattered between the beast's feet, lay pieces of a torn page.

## CHAPTER
# NINE

PAUL SLAMMED the sketchbook shut and stared at the wall, his breath coming in deep, strained huffs. His eyes blurred and then focused on the woodgrain patterns in the wallboards, the winding lines resembling the nearby forest highways or the shadows of the trees which hovered over the back of his house like a tarantula. The lines he had been drawing, he realized, were everywhere, pulled along by the strings of another's design.

*Stop it. You're acting crazy. Just finish the damn drawing.*

He opened the sketchbook, flipping past the first page without looking. He glimpsed through the other historical interpretations with bated breath before returning to his own work in progress. If he could just finish this, he could pay his mortgage,

replace his window, and turn on his heat. After this
...

*A paycheck, a scotch, and a shrink.*

He picked up the pencil and resumed his illustration, touching up the eyes, seasoning them with a dash of humanity. Tracing delicate hairs along the beast's hide. Shading to add depth and dimension, while maintaining The Society's commercial style. As he drew, the corners of his mouth formed the makings of a maniacal smile, one which he thought might resemble a mad scientist in the hour of his discovery.

But a heavy fatigue crept upon him like a spell, and before he could finish, his eyelids drooped and then closed. He fought them open three or four times before his arm lowered softly to the desk, his head turned sideways to rest upon the Wolfman's chest. Too tired to lift his head, he felt his mind begin to drift.

---

*Knock, knock.*

Paul's eyes forced themselves open. Slowly, he lifted his head in a state of confusion.

*Knock, knock, knock.*

He looked around, realizing what must have happened. As exhausted as he had been, he'd fallen asleep in the middle of his work, sleeping the entire night away. A dabble of drool blurred the drawing where his head had rested for the night. In a panic, he blotted it with his sweater. The illustration was nearly complete. He just needed to finish the lower legs and do some touch-ups to the—

*Bang, bang, bang.*

Paul jumped to his feet and glanced through the unbroken window on the left. It was dark outside. It wasn't morning after all. Goosebumps raced over his flesh.

*Who is knocking at my door in the middle of the night?*

He ran down the hallway to his bedroom, where he dropped to the floor and snatched his double-pump shotgun from beneath his bed. Just in case.

*Bang, bang.*

Paul raced to the front door. He usually kept his shotgun loaded, but he checked the barrel anyway along the way. He pumped it, took a deep breath, and looked through the peephole. His jaw fell open.

Clive Murkin stood outside, his face expressionless.

Paul held the gun down at his side and pulled open the door.

Four others stood flanking Clive in a silent V-formation, three men and one woman, their breath steaming in unison. Their long, dark coats contrasted with the porch-lit snow at their feet.

"I don't think that will be necessary," Clive said, gesturing to Paul's shotgun.

Paul could only imagine how he must have looked—exhausted and shocked, wearing clothes from the day before. "Wh–what's going on? Why did you c–come here in the middle of the night?"

Clive lifted an arm, sliding the sleeve of his overcoat to reveal a golden watch. He checked the time, frowning as if he hadn't considered the hour. "We came to check on you, Paul. Based on your words, I was expecting your illustration yesterday."

"There was a setback," Paul blurted. "The wind smashed one of my windows and … it set me behind." He ran a hand through his hair. "But I'm nearly finished, now."

"Good. The Society does not tolerate dawdlers, Mr. Desmontes." He turned his head to address his cohorts. "Do we?" They shook their heads and he turned back to Paul. "It's important to stay on task. Understood?"

"Yes. You'll get the final sketch today."

The pin sunk into his chest like a fang, pulling his attention downward, and he gasped.

"We'll be waiting," said Clive. His voice sounded distant.

When Paul looked back up, they had turned away, though he still felt their eyes upon him. They left in the same formation, their trench coat tails leaving slug-lines in the snow. Clive darted away, down the center, to resume his position at the head of the group. The snow crunched thickly beneath their boots, loud in the stillness of the night. Overhead, a crescent moon hung in a dark, starless sky.

The pin dug deeper and Paul winced. He shut the door, and bolted it, his hands shaking. Halfway down the hall, his skin began to crawl. Something was wrong. He rubbed at the site of the pin and reflected on his unwelcome visitors—The Society. At last, he realized what was bothering him.

*Not one of them was wearing a pin.*

# CHAPTER
# TEN

PAUL FLOATED dream-like through the icy hall and slumped back into the chair. His hands were empty. Somewhere along the way, he had dropped the shotgun, though he never heard it hit the floor. Outside, the wind howled, shifting the wood buffer and straining the tape around the edges. No light came from the other window—only the darkness of night. His breath steamed as an unseen force pulled his wrist upward. He held the pencil delicately, not recalling having lifted it, and the tip found his sketchpad. The motion was fluid, like a concerto, as he picked up where he had left off, stroking the Wolfman into magnificent creation.

A woman's mournful visage emerged, floating like a phantom inside his head. It was Serafina from the market.

*"It's happening again,"* she said. *"Please, take off the pin!"*

Paul ignored her. She was only a hallucination, and his masterpiece was nearly complete. How wrong he had been about The Elite Illustration Society! He understood their grand vision now. It was funny how outlooks change. Funny how, on one day, you could feel overtly passionate about one side of an argument, only to flip it around the next.

He rotated the pencil to add clefts of fur to the creature's feet and to add shade under the beast's eyes, which seemed more and more to look straight at him. After several minutes, it was all done, aside from some final touches. Now, he would flip back through the earlier depictions to see if there was anything he might have missed.

Serafina's face twisted in agony. She frowned, begging. *"The pin, Nigel ... take it off!"*

"I'm not your brother!" he screamed, and the vision scattered like dust.

But her interference had broken Paul's trance, and he recognized a power other than himself in the room. Something that drove not only his body, but also his thoughts and desires. Goosebumps flashed over his scalp, across his arms, and down his legs. With effort, he willed the pencil from his grip. It fell, bouncing on the desk, and he jumped to his feet. A sharp bite at his chest had him rip the pin from his sweater and fling it across the room. His pain fell away with the pin, which clattered and rolled across the floor. His fingers found the skin beneath where the pin had been, but there was no wound.

*It was a phantom pain. Now that I've taken the pin off, it's lost control over me.*

"This is over now!" Paul proclaimed, kicking the back of his chair into his desk. "You hear me?? I'm through with all of this."

Paul turned, took two steps toward the door and—

Something threw him to the chair with tremendous force.

Paul groaned, and his breath caught in his throat. He tried to stand but could not. The armrests held his arms, as if bound by invisible rope. The pages of the sketchbook flipped back one-by-one. All depictions were the same as the first Wolfman now. Each one locked eyes with Paul, sending a chill down his spine.

Nosferatu spoke to him from the other room. *Did you think Clive hired you for your talent, Paul?*

He could sense the vampire's smile. Struggling in his chair, he tried to plead with the clock. But an unseen force held his jaw shut.

*He didn't,* suggested the vampire. *He selected you*

*for your weakness and insecurity. You are prey, Paul. You always have been.*

Paul screamed with his mouth closed, and a deliberate wind flipped the pages back to the last drawing. His illustration was the same as the others now, with one difference. A vast symbol, like an eye over a dangling hook, throbbed at the center of the page. A moment later, the page tore free and shot upward, drifting behind him. Then the sketchbook flipped to the first page, where the Wolfman still stood with the torn bits of paper at his feet, before fading entirely.

A crackling of fire from behind seized Paul's breath and the chair spun him around, making him dizzy. At the center of the room, where his pin had landed, the torn page was ablaze. Beneath the flames, a giant eye appeared, sketched on the floor in charred and pulsating lines. Paul recognized it as the symbol he had seen moments before in his sketchbook. The eye grew in the room until its pupil was large enough to swallow a man, and it sank, forming a pit in the middle of the room.

A claw reached up from the depths and clutched the edge.

Paul screamed until his throat burned. He jerked from side to side in the chair and kicked at the floor, trying desperately to break free. But the unseen force held him in its grip.

*No, no ... I took it off! I took off the pin!!*

A second claw emerged and the beast leapt up from the abyss. It towered in the room, saliva dripping and hissing like acid as it struck the floor. It found Paul squirming in his chair and locked him in its feral gaze. Its long, gnarled tongue sprung like a vine from its mouth, twisting in the icy air and whipping its snout in ravenous hunger.

The unseen thing held Paul's eyes open.

*Oh God, this can't be real!*

The creature's rumbling snarl shook the floorboards, chilling Paul's blood. It bared its dagger-like teeth and gums, sending spittle dancing around its maw and flying across the room. The vile fluid struck Paul's face and burned, sliding down his cheeks and trembling neck. The beast's hot breath found Paul's nostrils, and he retched, his stomach muscles twisting to knots at the ghastly stench. The Wolfman turned its snout up and howled, sending Paul's hairs on end. Three grey wolves emerged from the pit, one after the other, following their master toward its prey.

Paul jerked and kicked in his chair, sobbing and contorting, bound by the unseen. At last, sweating in the freezing air, his eyes wet with tears, his lips parted enough to allow his final cry. The desperate, high-pitched scream of human prey.

Outside, the sun showed its first light. The last

thing Paul Desmontes saw before the Wolfman sank its teeth deep into his skull was Clive Murkin. The Head of The Society watched him through the window, with a wide, impish grin on his face.

# PLEASE LEAVE A REVIEW

If you've enjoyed Death Sketch, please leave a review at the product page where you purchased this e-book. Goodreads is also a great place to leave a review.

Reviews help authors get more eyes on their books, which is important to building an author's career. Long story short ... reviews allow me to write more books!

# FURTHER NIGHTMARES...

Want to know more of the "why" behind Death Sketch?

A companion story on the ancestry of Clive Murkin and the Wolfman is in the works, slated for release in late 2024.

Join The Youngblood Newsletter to receive updates on that story, as well as the next all-new entry in the Nightmares series, also set to come out in 2024.

Sign up at https://www.tobiasyoungblood.com/

The newsletter is completely free to sign up and you'll never be spammed by me. You can opt out at any time.

# ABOUT THE AUTHOR

Tobias Youngblood lives in Coastal Virginia, where he grew up inspired by the likes of Stephen King, Ursula K. Le Guin, Robert Heinlein, Clive Barker, and J.R.R. Tolkien, to name a few. He loves the Alien movies, the Thing, and The Fly, and most dark mashups of sci-fi, fantasy, and horror. His own work tends to a variety of speculative fiction which blends these elements.

Tobias is set to complete the Projectionists urban fantasy trilogy in 2024. He is also hard at work on a Nightmares series of short horror fiction with co-author Oliver Shade. Several sci-fi works are also in the pipeline.

Made in the USA
Monee, IL
29 July 2025

22162170R00042